JE

C22286

Flora, J.
Joking man

3.30

Date		Due	

CASS COUNTY PUBLIC LIBRARY

**Peculiar Branch
Peculiar, Mo.**

P

Story and pictures by

JAMES FLORA

HARCOURT, BRACE & WORLD, INC.

NEW YORK

P.

C22286

Other books by James Flora

THE FABULOUS FIREWORK FAMILY
THE DAY THE COW SNEEZED
CHARLIE YUP AND HIS SNIP-SNAP BOYS
KANGAROO FOR CHRISTMAS
LEOPOLD, THE SEE-THROUGH CRUMBPICKER
MY FRIEND CHARLIE
GRANDPA'S FARM
SHERWOOD WALKS HOME
FISHING WITH DAD

FOR MARGARET

Library of Congress Catalog Card Number: 68-25185
Printed in the United States of America
First edition

ur town was a grumpy place before the joking man came. We didn't have much fun except when we went swimming or played baseball or tickled each other.

Every day was just like the day before, and we all knew that it would be just like tomorrow, too.

The joking man changed all of that.

He made us laugh. Even the grumpiest people learned to cackle and giggle that summer.

It all started with the rubber park bench. It looked just like all of the other benches in Courthouse Park until you sat on it.

If you sat down hard, as I did, it would zing you into the air like a big slingshot.

If you sat down easy, like my friend Charlie, you would sink slowly down to the ground.

Fat Mrs. Kelty sank all of the way down and couldn't get up. Three men from the courthouse had to help her.

Mr. Frisbie sat so hard that he shot across the path into the bushes and his hat flew up a tree. Charlie had to climb up and fetch it for him.

Before the day was over, most everybody in town was hiding behind the trees in the park—waiting to see who would be next to sit on the rubber bench.

That night Charlie and I went to the movies. In the middle of the picture, just when the Indians were chasing the cowboys, somebody let loose thousands of moths. And you know what moths do. They all try to crowd into the light.

You have never seen such a crazy sight. It was like being inside a big light bulb full of birds.

People began to giggle and laugh. It wasn't a very good movie, but people roared and howled. You would have thought it was the funniest movie ever made.

We were still laughing when we came out of the theater,
and we laughed even harder when we found that somebody
had put square wheels on the mayor's car. He drove home
with his hat bouncing in the air.

We knew then that we had a joking man in town.

Who was he?

Nobody knew. Nobody could say.

You can see that it began to get very exciting in our town. Charlie and I hated to go to bed for fear we would miss one of the joking man's tricks.

One morning I woke up to hear people running down the street shouting to each other:

"Hurry! Hurry! The bank is selling money cheap!"

I got out of bed and ran to the bank, too. There was a big sign over the door. It said:

SPECIAL — TODAY ONLY
FRESH NEW DOLLAR BILLS ONLY 49¢ EACH

There must have been a thousand people there waiting for
the bank to open so they could buy some of that cheap money.

Mr. Hershey, the bank manager, finally put his head out
of the window and said, "I'm sorry about this, folks. We're not
having a money sale today. It's just another of the joking
man's jokes."

People started to grumble. They felt cheated, and some
were getting mad. There might have been trouble if just then
Mr. Tooley, the milkman, hadn't run down the street screeching, "What no-good, lardheaded joker painted all of my
cows?"

Of course we all forgot about the bank and rushed over to Mr. Tooley's pasture to see the cows.

Let me tell you, they were a sight for sore eyes.

Every one of Mr. Tooley's cows had been painted with different designs and colors.

Some cows had stripes.

Some had polka dots and squiggles.

Some had faces and some had clothes painted on them. One was painted like a checkerboard, and another was covered with flowers.

It was so gorgeous and silly that people began to giggle and squawk with laughter.

Charlie and I had planned to go fishing that day, but the cows were so pretty that we just sat there admiring them. Every once in a while I would say to Charlie, "Just tell me when and where you've ever seen prettier cows than these cows."

"Never. Anywhere," Charlie would answer. "Why, these cows are so beautiful, they should be hung in the Metropolitan Museum of Art."

Then we would roll in the grass and laugh until our sides ached. Charlie has a good sense of humor. So do I.

The joking man must have seen how we all enjoyed his tricks. It made him work harder. Jokes began coming so fast that we would just finish laughing at one joke when we would have to start laughing at another.

While Judge O'Malley was on his vacation, the joking man put a whole automobile in his office. Charlie and I figured that the joking man carried it in piece by piece and put it together. There just didn't seem to be any other way to get that big old car in that little bitty office.

When the judge got back from his trip and found that car, he was fit to be tied. He raved and ranted. He vowed as how he would hang the joking man by his heels if he ever found him.

He was so mad that he got in the car and drove it right through the wall of his office. We ran home and hid. We didn't think that was such a funny joke after all.

It didn't seem to bother the joking man, though. The next day he was back at work again. He put sails on all of the ducks on the town pond. Of course everybody went down to see those ducks sailing around like big yachts.

Suddenly a huge sea monster reared out of the water.

It very nearly scared everybody half to death.

You have never seen such scrambling or heard such screeching. They all took off down the road like mice at a cat's picnic. They ran so fast that they lost their hats and shoes and false teeth.

They fetched the sheriff with his big shotgun.

BLAM! BLAM!

The monster fell back into the water. When the sheriff rowed out in a boat, he found that the monster was made of wood. A rope led from one end of it to a bunch of bushes on the other side of the pond.

The joking man had struck again.

The people who had been scared by the monster didn't think that it was a very funny trick, but Charlie and I did.

We like all kinds of jokes, no matter how scary they are.

We liked it when the joking man put soap suds in the tuba for the Fourth of July parade. Such nice bubbles.

We liked it at the town meeting when he tied some mice to balloons and floated them out over the stage. We liked it even better when he floated some cats out, too.

Everybody said that it was the best town meeting they could remember.

When Stanley Simpkins got a new swimming pool, he wouldn't let anybody swim in it. He wouldn't even let Charlie and me go wading.

The joking man must have heard how stingy Stanley was, so one night he filled that pool with jello. You should have heard the nice GLOP Stanley made when he dove in the next morning.

One rainy Sunday morning the people came out of church and put up their umbrellas.

SPLAP!

The joking man had struck again. He had gone into the cloakroom and filled their umbrellas with cold spaghetti.

It made those people very mad because they had to walk home with spaghetti hanging from their hats and noses.

Right then and there a lot of people began to think that the joking man wasn't funny any more.

But he made people even madder when he pulled his TV joke.

He called everybody who had a television set and said, "This is station KNUT. We are going to blow the soot out of all your television tubes this afternoon. Please take your television set out on the lawn so your house won't get dirty."

Charlie and I walked all over town that day. People were sitting outside in their oldest, dirtiest clothes looking at their TV sets. They didn't want to spoil their good clothes when the soot blew out.

When it got dark and no soot had appeared, they realized that the joking man had tricked them again. They didn't think it was funny at all. Most of them called the police and said they wanted the joking man arrested.

I guess that scared the joking man because he didn't play any more tricks until the first day of school.

The night before school opened, the joking man painted black all over the windows of the principal's house. When the principal woke in the morning, he could see that it was still night. So he turned over and went back to sleep.

Later he woke up and yawned. It was still dark outside.

"This is the longest night I can remember," he said as he went back to sleep.

Later the telephone rang. It was Miss Dailey, a teacher at the school.

"Aren't you feeling well?" she asked.

The principal yawned and snorted. "Why in tarnation are you calling me in the middle of the night to ask me how I feel?"

"It's not the middle of the night," Miss Dailey said. "It's eleven o'clock in the morning, and all of the children are waiting for you to start the new school year."

You can imagine how the principal roared and howled at that joking man joke. He called the police and yelled, "I want you to find that joking man and put him in jail *immediately*."

But the police couldn't do that.

They didn't know who he was or where to find him.

Nobody did.

I suppose all of that scared the joking man because he never played another joke.

Now our town is just as grumpy and grouchy as it was before the joking man came.

Charlie and I miss the joking man's tricks. We talk about him a lot and wish he would come back and do some more.

One day I said to Charlie, "I'll bet a dollar that you know who the joking man was."

"Sure I do," Charlie said. "And I'll bet a zillion dollars that you know, too."

"Of course I do." I laughed. "Do you suppose anybody else knows? Do you think the readers of this book know who the joking man was?"

"Not unless we tell them," Charlie said. "Shall we let them in on the secret?"

"Let's do it," I said. "If they will just turn the page, we'll show them a picture of the joking man."

There you are.

You can see that there wasn't just one joking man.

There were two joking boys: Charlie and me. We played all of those good tricks.

Now that you know our secret, I hope you'll never tell. But if you are the sort of person who can't keep a secret, I hope you'll only tell your mother or your very best friend.

Never, ever tell the principal.

You want Charlie and me to pass into the fourth grade, don't you?